S0-ARL-747

MY MIDDOS WORLD

My Middos World was first published in Hebrew in 1993 and immediately became a best seller. Tens of thousands of copies were sold, benefiting hundreds of educators and parents.

What makes this series so outstanding? Besides being so beautiful in every aspect – impressive pictures, special laminated paper, a large size format – the contents of the books are very special indeed. The stories are written in a simple manner, yet they convey a deep Jewish message. They portray the beauty of good middos from a Torah outlook and teach us to perform Mitzvos happily and wholeheartedly.

The books elicit the positive potential in every child and help him see the beauty in himself and in the Torah world surrounding him.

We hope that *My Middos World* will bring great enjoyment and benefit to young Jewish children throughout the world.

Published by:
Beckerman Publishers
19 Lubavitch St, Ramat Shlomo,
Jerusalem, 97520
Tel: (02)-5863796 Fax: (02)-5862598
Email:beckermn@bezeqint.net

Distributed by:
Israel Book Shop
501 Prospect St, Lakewood, NJ, 08701
Tel: (732)-901-3009
Fax: (732)-901-4012
Email: isrbkshp@aol.com

Printed in Israel

בס"ד

Menuchah Beckerman

Be Careful Michael!

14

Every morning when Michael wakes up, the first thing he does is wash 'negel-vasser'. He does not rub his eyes or play with his toys or walk around the house until his hands are pure of 'tum'ah'.

Mommy stands near Michael to make sure he washes properly. Usually, Michael does it just right. He knows that you first have to pour water from the cup onto the right hand, and then onto the left hand, then right, then left – three times altogether on each hand.

Sometimes, Mommy sees that the water did not cover his whole hand, and then Michael washes that hand again.

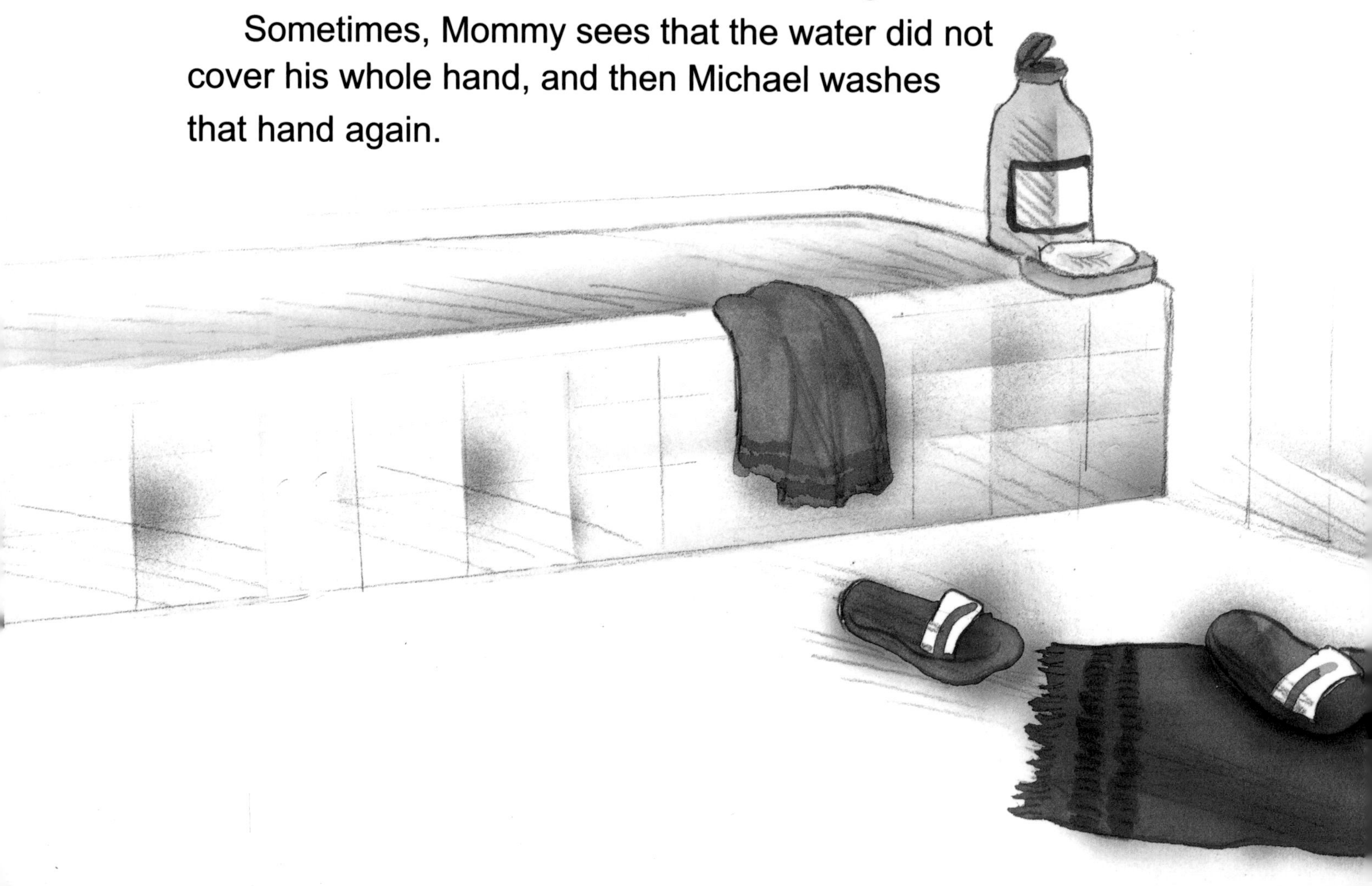

Next, Michael quickly gets dressed. The 'tzitzis' are easy to put on. One, two, three – and his head is in the hole. Smooth out the front and the back, and that's all there is to it! The shirt is a little harder for him to manage. Sometimes the buttons get mixed up, and the shirt comes out a little lopsided. Michael isn't lazy. He opens up all the buttons, straightens out the shirt, and buttons it up once more. He tries again and again, until finally, the shirt is buttoned properly.

Michael knows how to put on his shoes, too. He knows which shoe goes on the right foot, and which shoe goes on the left foot. He doesn't know how to tie his laces yet, so he goes to Mommy, picks his foot up on a chair – so that Mommy won't have to bend down – and Mommy ties it for him. Michael is always amazed how Mommy has the bow neatly tied in a second, before he can even blink!

Michael is a good boy. But sometimes good boys do silly things. Mischievous Michael likes to fool around on the way to Yeshiva.

Whenever he passes by the tall tree down the block, he climbs right up. He climbs and climbs, until he gets all the way to the tree-top. Then he shouts out loud for all to hear: “See how brave I am? I got to the top, and I’m not even afraid!” He ‘rides’ on the branch as if it is a horse.

In Shul, he climbs onto the banister and … whoops – he slides down to the bottom. He climbs on the gate in school, too. He even likes to climb on the railing of the porch in his house.

He would climb on to the stone wall outside, and prance about without holding on. Once, when his cousin Chani saw him doing it, she got real scared. She closed her eyes; she was afraid to even look at him!

"Michael, get down! It's dangerous! You can fall, 'chas v'sholom', and hurt yourself. It will hurt a lot, and even bleed!" she pleaded with him. But Michael just laughed, and told her: "You're a scaredy-cat, because you're just a little girl. I'm big already! I'm not afraid of anything!"

Michael was sure that doing dangerous things proved how big and brave he was.

But one day, Michael discovered that he was making a big mistake!

What happened that day?

It was on a Friday – that's Michael's favorite day in Yeshiva. The Rebbe tells a lot of interesting stories from the Parsha. Then he hands out a Parsha sheet – a paper with a nice picture to color, about the Parsha. At the end of class, right before they go home, he gives them each a treat, 'lechoved Shabbos' – something sweet - a cookie, or a lollipop, or a taffy.

The Rebbe has a very pleasant voice. He speaks softly and calmly. The children sit quietly, and listen closely to every word he says.

א ב ג ד ה ו ז ח
ט י כ ל מ נ ס ע
פ צ ק ר ש ת
ם ן

"This week's Parsha is called 'Ki-Setzeh,'" the Rebbe said. "In the Parsha, it says that every Yid must make a 'ma'akeh' around his roof. What is a 'ma'akeh?' It is a railing, or a low wall, around a high place. You must put a 'ma'akeh' around the roof, otherwise, someone standing at the edge of the roof might, 'chas v'sholom', fall down.

"Why don't we fall down when we stand on a porch or a fire escape?" the Rebbe asked.

"Because the porch has a 'ma'akeh' around it!" answered Yisroel Meir.

"Very good," nodded the Rebbe. "If there would be no railing, a person could slip off. It's very dangerous to fall from a high place.

"I'm going to tell you a story that is a little sad, but listen well, it will teach you how important it is not to do dangerous things!

"There was once a little boy named Yankele who was very mischievous. He loved to climb in high, dangerous places. Yankele thought he was very brave. He wasn't afraid of anything.

"One time, when Yankele climbed up a tall tree, the branch snapped off, and he fell

and broke his foot. He cried hard, because it hurt a lot.

"Five long weeks, he lay in the hospital. After that, for a whole year, he limped on that foot and he had to walk around with a cane like an old man.

"Poor Yankele! All that year, he couldn't run and play. He could hardly climb up the steps. His foot hurt him all the time.

"Why did it all happen? Because he was so mischievous," concluded the Rebbe.

Michael raised his hand and asked: "What if somebody is big, and really, truly brave – is he allowed to climb in high places?"

"Definitely not," answered the Rebbe. "Even adults can fall down. Somebody who is really grown up understands the mitzvah of 'Venishmartem me'od lenafshoseichem', 'Take very good care of yourself.' It's an aveirah to do dangerous things.

"You kinderlach are all little tzaddikim. I am sure that you are all very careful. Tell me, boys, what things should we watch out for?" asked the Rebbe.

"We're not allowed to go near fire, or to play with matches," called out Berel.

"We don't play with pins or needles. They can hurt us!" Chaim jumped up and answered. (Just yesterday, he had played with Mommy's sewing needles, and he had cut his finger.)

"We're not allowed to play in the street! Cars go there!" explained Yisroel Meir.

"Children shouldn't use sharp knives!" said Shmuli.

"We shouldn't walk near pits. We can fall in and hurt ourselves!" added Michael. (On Lag B'Omer, he had fallen into a pit.)

"We're not allowed to take medicine by ourselves," said Avi. (He had read a beautiful story about it, so he knew how dangerous it is.)

"We're not allowed to go near wild dogs. They can bite us," called out Michael excitedly. (He once went shopping with his Mommy, and they saw a big scary dog.)

"We're not allowed to throw stones!" shouted Motty. (Tatty warned him about that many times.)

The Rebbe smiled and said: "I see that I was right. You are all big and smart. You know all about dangerous things, and you know how to stay away from them!"

Then they all sang songs, and before going home, the Rebbe gave each child a lollipop and a Parsha sheet.

Michael ran home. He wanted to show Mommy the nice pictures on his paper - a house with a ma'akeh around the roof, and a big pit with a fence around it.

On the way home Michael met Yitzik, his cute little neighbor who was two and a half years old. Yitzik was holding a big ball in his hands.

Suddenly, the ball rolled out into the busy street.

Little Yitzik did not stop to think. He ran into the street. Luckily, Michael was there. He grabbed little Yitzik, held his hand tightly, and told him: “Yitzik, there’s a car coming! Don’t go into the street. It’s dangerous.

“You are a very cute little boy, but you don’t understand. I’m big and I know that it is a Mitzvah to take care of ourselves. My Rebbi told me all about it! Hold my hand and do as I say.”

The two boys waited on the sidewalk. Michael saw an adult neighbor passing by. He asked him to please get the ball. The neighbor looked to the right and to the left and then to the right again. He waited until he was absolutely sure that there were no cars, and then he carefully went into the street, picked up the ball, and handed it to Yitzik.

“You see! This is how we should take care of ourselves. You should never go into the street until it’s really safe.” Michael felt very smart.

Michael and Yitzik walked home holding hands. Michael didn’t let go of Yitzik’s hand - not even for a second. He was afraid that his little friend would jump into the street again.

When Michael brought Yitzik to his Mommy, she was thrilled. "Thank you Michael! Thank you very much. I was very worried about Yitzik. He disappeared a few minutes ago. I looked for him but I couldn't find him. You are big and smart, Michael. You took good care of my baby!" Michael was very proud of himself. It felt good to do a Mitzvah!

Suddenly Michael noticed that the lollipop which the Rebbe had given him was missing!

Then he remembered. When he had run to catch Yitzik, the lollipop had fallen out of his hand into the street.

Michael was sad, because a lollipop from the Rebbe has a special taste. But when he glanced at Yitzik again, all of his sadness disappeared. Yitzik smiled at him, as if to say: 'Thank you for taking good care of me!' Michael felt good inside. He felt that taking care of a baby is worth more than a hundred lollipops.

Michael patted Yitzik, and then he said good-bye and went home. He hurried to show his Mommy his beautiful picture and to tell her that she could depend on him from now on. She need not worry about him any more, because he would never do anything dangerous.

Michael was very happy to be such a lucky boy. It's great to be a Yid! Michael felt good that he was able to learn Torah and to keep the mitzvos properly.